1

Dancing on the Moon

Written by Janice Roper

Illustrated by Lauren Grimm

SIDS Educational Services ◇ Cheverly, Maryland

This book was made possible with generous funding from the Center for Infant and Child Loss, University of Maryland, Baltimore Campus, 630 West Fayette, Room 568, Baltimore, MD 21201, 800-808-SIDS (800-808-7437).

Order additional copies or sponsor books for low income families. A tax-deductible $100 donation sponsors six books and includes a dedication to your loved one on thc inside cover. What a wonderful tribute to someone you love. Visa/Mastercard accepted.

To order additional copies: SIDS Educational Services, 2905 64th Avenue, Cheverly, MD 20785
Call toll-free: **877 We Love You (877-935-6839)** or 301-322-2620   Fax: 301-322-9822

Dancing on the Moon Text copyright © 2001 by Janice Roper.
Illustrations copyright © 2001 by Lauren Grimm.

Publisher's Cataloging-in-Publication
(provided by Quality Books, Inc.)

Roper, Janice.
    Dancing on the moon / written by Janice Roper ;
Illustrated by Lauren Grimm. — 1st ed.
    p. cm.
    SUMMARY: A young girl experiences jealousy when her brother is born, then anxiety and sadness when he dies. In a dream she flies to the moon to bring him back and make her parents happy again.
    Audience: Ages 3-8
    ISBN 0-9641218-6-7
        Printed in Korea
    1. Jealousy in children—Juvenile fiction.
2. Brothers and sisters—Juvenile fiction. 3. Dreams – Juvenile fiction. I. Grimm, Lauren. II. Title.

PZ7.R67885Dan 2001   [E]
        QB100-901633

Special Thanks

Special thanks to my husband Bruce, my living children Selena, Marisa, and Robin, my sisters Kathryn & Jennifer, my brothers, Mom, Dad, the Greens, the Ropers, Mary K, Adam, Sue & Brian Benson, Virginia & Frank Harris, Jan Viar, Martha Marani, Wanda Rizer, Cheryl Radich, Joani Horchler, Chuck & Deb Mihalko, my co-workers, friends, extended family, and CICL who rallied around me with such love and support when I really needed it.

Also thanks to Donna Becker, Jean Edwards, Pat Hand and Chuck Dohrman.

This book is dedicated to Danny Roper, Kellyn Schaefer, Emily Harris, Christian Horchler, Laura Turner, Nigel Radich, PJ Buth, Whitney Figliozzi, Isaiah Green, Meg Mihalko, Zachary Dorhman, Carly Hollander, Megan Biebel, and all of the children whose short lives continue to touch us so deeply and beautifully.
— J.R.

For Mike, Keeley, and Sean
— L.G.

Carly was five when Nigel came home

Mom cuddled
him often
and left her alone

She crawled on her lap,
tried to push him aside

But Mommy held tight,
and the baby just cried.

Carly fiddled with dolls,
then stamped her
right shoe

"Mommy!" she yelled,
"Play with me too!"

Mommy smiled a sweet smile and gave her a hug

she put Nigel down on the big center rug

She picked Carly up and cradled her face

Saying: "Both of my babies brighten this place."

"You bring sunshine and Nigel the moon

"I love you so much that
it fills up this room!

"Daddy and you and
Nigel and me

"Are connected by love
like branches to a tree

"We will always
be together,
even when we're apart

"Both of my babies
are here in my heart."

Then Carly was happy, she gave Nigel a kiss

Saying: "You are my brother and I'm your big Sis!"

They played through each day and Nigel he grew

Carly tickled his neck and made him say "Coo"

But one cold rainy day, Carly heard a sharp scream

Then crying and yelling, about Nigel it seemed

Then they took him away
and Mommy went too

In an ambulance with lights
and sounds like "whoo whoo!"

Mrs. Viar came over but the day was so long
Carly cried because Mommy and Nigel were gone

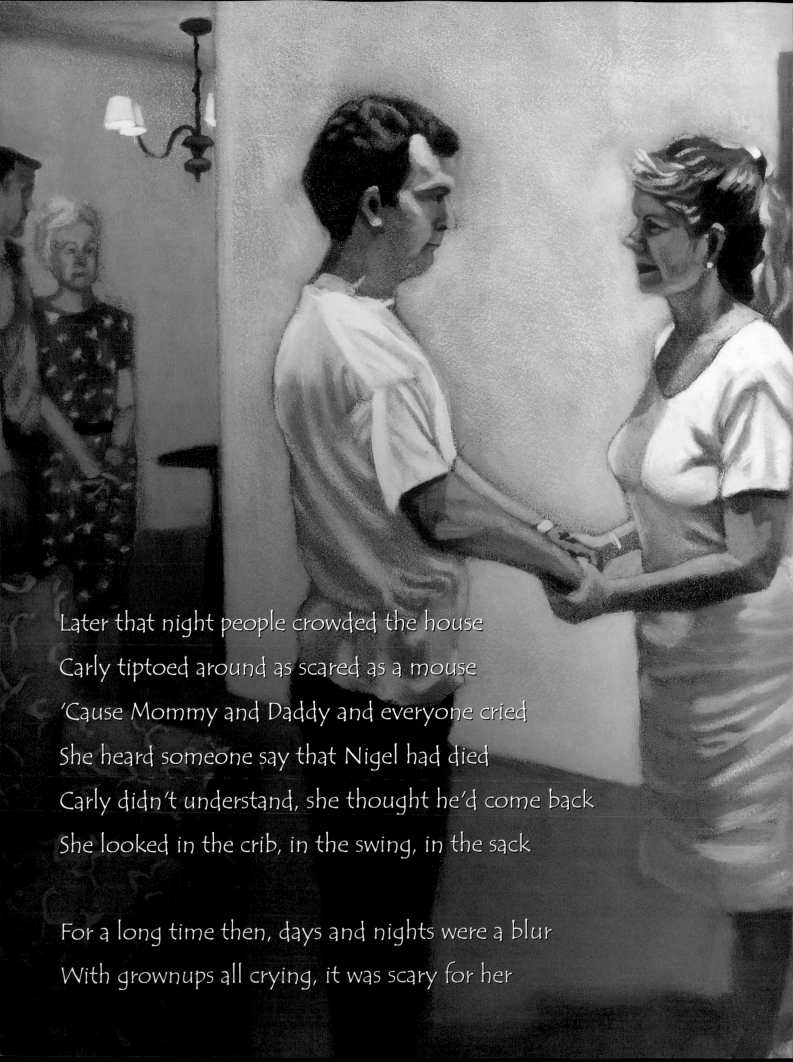

Later that night people crowded the house

Carly tiptoed around as scared as a mouse

'Cause Mommy and Daddy and everyone cried

She heard someone say that Nigel had died

Carly didn't understand, she thought he'd come back

She looked in the crib, in the swing, in the sack

For a long time then, days and nights were a blur

With grownups all crying, it was scary for her

To bring Nigel home,
she wanted so badly

To kiss his fat cheeks and
tickle him gladly

To make Mommy happy,
to see Daddy smile

To have little
Nigel back,
just for a
while

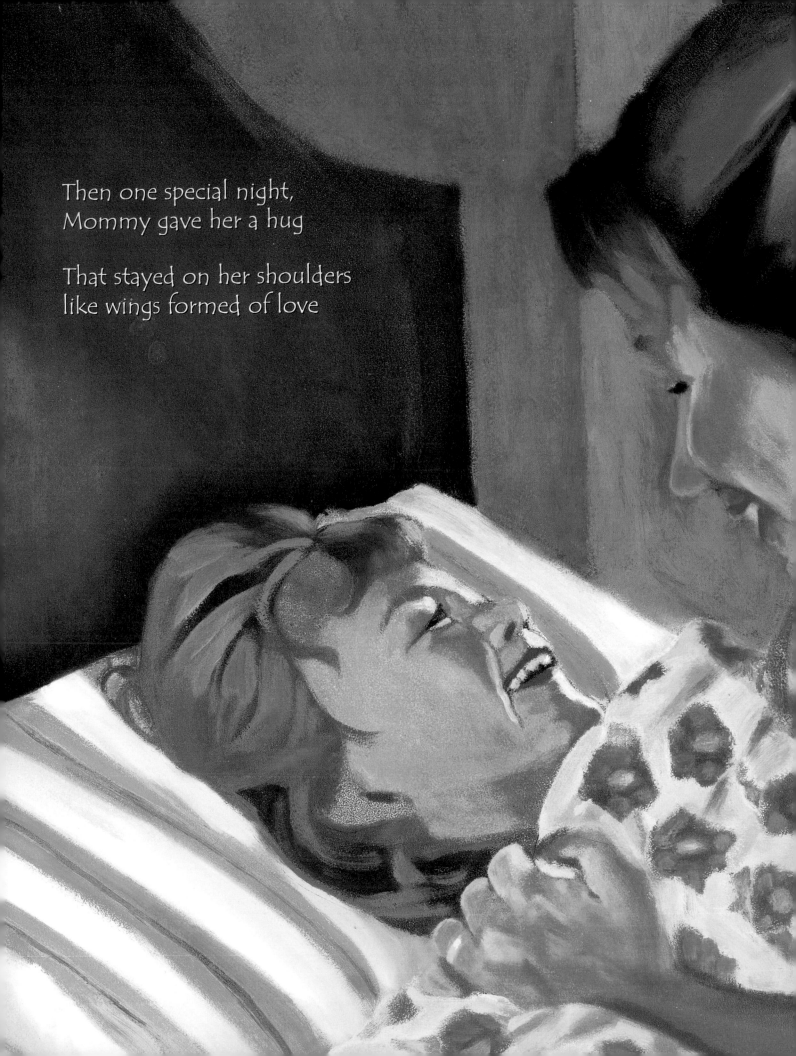

Then one special night,
Mommy gave her a hug

That stayed on her shoulders
like wings formed of love

The moon was full and bright on that night

And with her new wings, little Carly took flight

She flew and she flew,
straight for the moon's face

She landed and looked
all over the place

She squealed when she saw a small little guy
        Saying:

"Nigel! I found you! Up high in the sky!

"Come home right now, Mom and Dad have been sick!

"Come home with me now!
        Come home with me quick!"

Carly kissed his fat cheeks and hugged him so hard
Nigel laughed, his eyes sparkled, and shone with the stars

"My Carly," he said
(because now
he could talk)

"I rest on your shoulder
                as you take a walk

"I am threads in the shirt you
pull over your head

"I am soft fluffy blankets
that hug you in bed

"When you feel the wind,
I am stroking your hair

"I will stay with you always,
and be everywhere!"

She picked up her Nigel
and they swung in the air

And danced on the moon
with nary a care

They laughed and they twirled on the moon's rocky face

But soon Carly knew she must leave this place

"Come with me!" She begged, "I've got to go home."

"The house is so quiet and sad since you've gone."

Nigel smiled a sweet smile and reached up his hands

Carly carried him far across those strange lands

Then at the moon's edge,
when she knew they must part

She hugged him so hard...

he slipped into her heart.

Carly woke up with blankets so warm in her room

She looked out her window and...*there was the moon!*

Soon came her Mommy,
Carly held her so tight

It was then that she knew,
her Mommy was right.

Nigel's not gone, he was inside her heart

And from that day forward
they were never apart.

About the Author

Mrs. Roper is an Account Manager for an internet technology firm full-time — and a poet part-time. She lives in Annapolis. Maryland, with her husband Bruce, and her three surviving daughters: Selena, Marisa and Robin. XZ

Left to right: Lauren Grimm, illustrator; Selena Roper; and Janice Roper, author.

About the Illustrator

Lauren Grimm received her M.F.A in Painting at Colorado State University, and her B.S. in Art Education at the University of Vermont. A former art teacher, Lauren now paints in her home studio. *Dancing on the Moon* is her first children's picture book. Lauren lives in Vienna, Virginia, with her husband Mike and two children Sean and Keeley.

About the Designer

Wanda Rizer is an award-winning designer of both print and multi-media web sites. A long-time friend of Mrs. Roper, she generously donated her time and talent in the layout and production for *Dancing on the Moon*. She owns the firm Design4Impact.com and lives in Abbottstown, Pennsylvania, with her husband, Michael, and their two companion parrots: Mac, and Albert E.